THE RAILWAY STORIES
The Rev. W. Awdry

THE THREE RAILWAY ENGINES

JAMES THE RED ENGINE

TROUBLESOME ENGINES

WITH ILLUSTRATIONS BY

C. REGINALD DALBY

This edition first published in Great Britain in 1982 by
Octopus Books Limited
59 Grosvenor Street
London W1

The Three Railway Engines first published in Great Britain
in 1945 by Edmund Ward (Publishers) Ltd
Copyright 1945 Edmund Ward (Publishers) Ltd
Copyright © 1967 Kaye & Ward Ltd
James the Red Engine first published in Great Britain
in 1948 by Edmund Ward (Publishers) Ltd 1948
Copyright 1948 Edmund Ward (Publishers) Ltd
Copyright © 1970 Kaye & Ward Ltd
Troublesome Engines first published in Great Britain
in 1950 by Edmund Ward (Publishers) Ltd 1950
Copyright © 1950 Edmund Ward (Publishers) Ltd
Copyright © 1970 Kaye & Ward Ltd

ISBN 0 86273 053 8

Produced by
Mandarin Publishers Limited
22a Westlands Road,
Quarry Bay, Hong Kong

Printed in Hong Kong

THE RAILWAY STORIES

CONTENTS

THE THREE RAILWAY ENGINES

JAMES THE RED ENGINE

TROUBLESOME ENGINES

THE THREE RAILWAY ENGINES

EDWARD'S DAY OUT

Once upon a time there was a little engine called Edward. He lived in a shed with five other engines. They were all bigger than Edward and boasted about it. "The Driver won't choose you again," they said. "He wants big, strong engines like us." Edward had not been out for a long time; he began to feel sad.

Just then the Driver and Fireman came along to start work.

The Driver looked at Edward. "Why are you sad?" he asked. "Would you like to come out today?"

"Yes, please," said Edward. So the Fireman lit the fire and made a nice lot of steam.

Then the Driver pulled the lever, and Edward puffed away.

"Peep, peep," he whistled. "Look at me now."

The others were very cross at being left behind.

Away went Edward to get some coaches.

"Be careful, Edward," said the coaches, "don't bump and bang us like the other engines do." So Edward came up to the coaches, very, very gently, and the shunter fastened the coupling.

"Thank you, Edward," said the coaches. "That was kind, we are glad you are taking us today."

Then they went to the station where the people were waiting.

"Peep, peep," whistled Edward – "get in quickly, please."

So the people got in quickly and Edward waited happily for the Guard to blow his whistle, and wave his green flag.

He waited and waited – there was no whistle, no green flag. "Peep, peep, peep, peep – where is that Guard?" Edward was getting anxious.

The Driver and Fireman asked the Station Master, "Have you seen the Guard?" "No," he said. They asked the porter, "Have you seen the Guard?" "Yes – last night," said the porter.

Edward began to get cross. "Are we ever going to start?" he said.

Just then a little boy shouted, "Here he comes!" and there the Guard was, running down the hill with his flags in one hand and a sandwich in the other.

He ran on to the platform, blew his whistle, and jumped into his van.

Edward puffed off. He did have a happy day. All the children ran to wave as he went past and he met old friends at all the stations. He worked so hard that the Driver promised to take him out again next day.

"I'm going out again tomorrow," he told the other engines that night in the shed. "What do you think of that?"

But he didn't hear what they thought, for he was so tired and happy that he fell asleep at once.

EDWARD AND GORDON

One of the engines in Edward's shed was called Gordon. He was very big and very proud.

"You watch me this afternoon, little Edward," he boasted, "as I rush through with the express; that will be a splendid sight for you."

Just then his Driver pulled the lever. "Goodbye, little Edward," said Gordon, as he puffed away, "look out for me this afternoon!"

Edward went off, too, to do some shunting.

Edward liked shunting. It was fun playing with trucks. He would come up quietly and give them a pull.

"Oh! Oh! Oh! Oh! Oh!" screamed the trucks. "Whatever is happening?"

Then he would stop and the silly trucks would go bump into each other. "Oh! Oh! Oh! Oh!" they cried again.

Edward pushed them until they were running nicely, and when they weren't expecting it he would stop; one of them would be sure to run on to another line. Edward played till there were no more trucks; then he stopped to rest.

Presently he heard a whistle. Gordon came puffing along, very slowly, and very crossly. Instead of nice shining coaches, he was pulling a lot of very dirty coal trucks.

"A goods train! a goods train! a goods train!" he grumbled. "The shame of it, the shame of it, the shame of it."

He went slowly through, with the trucks clattering and banging behind him.

Edward laughed, and went to find some more trucks.

Soon afterwards a porter came and spoke to his Driver. "Gordon can't get up the hill. Will you take Edward and push him, please?"

They found Gordon halfway up the hill and very cross. His Driver and Fireman were talking to him severely. "You are not trying!" they told him.

"I can't do it," said Gordon. "The noisy trucks hold an engine back so. If they were coaches now – clean sensible things that come quietly – that would be different."

Edward's Driver came up. "We've come to push," he said. "No use at all," said Gordon. "You wait and see," said Edward's Driver.

They brought the train back to the bottom of the hill. Edward came up behind the brake van ready to push.

"Peep, peep, I'm ready," said Edward.

"Poop, poop, no good," grumbled Gordon.

The Guard blew his whistle and they pulled and pushed as hard as they could.

"I can't do it, I can't do it, I can't do it," puffed Gordon.

"I will do it, I will do it, I will do it," puffed Edward.

"I can't do it, I will do it, I can't do it, I will do it, I can't do it, I will do it," they puffed together.

Edward pushed and puffed and puffed and pushed, as hard as ever he could, and almost before he realized it, Gordon found himself at the top of the hill.

"I've done it! I've done it! I've done it!" he said proudly, and forgot all about Edward pushing behind. He didn't wait to say "Thank you", but ran on so fast that he passed two stations before his Driver could make him stop.

Edward had pushed so hard that when he got to the top he was out of breath.

Gordon ran on so fast that Edward was left behind.

The Guard waved and waved, but Edward couldn't catch up.

He ran on to the next station, and there the Driver and Fireman said they were very pleased with him. The Fireman gave him a nice long drink of water, and the Driver said, "I'll get out my paint tomorrow, and give you a beautiful new coat of blue with red stripes, then you'll be the smartest engine in the shed."

THE SAD STORY OF HENRY

Once, an engine attached to a train
Was afraid of a few drops of rain —

—It went into a tunnel,
And squeaked through its funnel
And never came out again.

The engine's name was Henry. His Driver and Fireman argued with him, but he would not move. "The rain will spoil my lovely green paint and red stripes," he said.

The Guard blew his whistle till he had no more breath, and waved his flags till his arms ached; but Henry still stayed in the tunnel, and blew steam at him.

"I am not going to spoil my lovely green paint and red stripes for you," he said rudely.

The passengers came and argued too, but Henry would not move.

A Fat Director who was on the train told the Guard to get a rope. "We will pull you out," he said. But Henry only blew steam at him and made him wet.

They hooked the rope on and all pulled – except the Fat Director. "My doctor has forbidden me to pull," he said.

They pulled and pulled and pulled, but still Henry stayed in the tunnel.

Then they tried pushing from the other end. The Fat Director said, "One, two, three, push": but did not help. "My doctor has forbidden me to push," he said.

They pushed and pushed and pushed; but still Henry stayed in the tunnel.

At last another train came. The Guard waved his red flag and stopped it. The two Engine Drivers, the two Firemen, and the two Guards went and argued with Henry. "Look, it has stopped raining," they said. "Yes, but it will begin again soon," said Henry. "And what would become of my green paint with red stripes then?"

So they brought the other engine up, and it pushed and puffed, and puffed and pushed as hard as ever it could. But still Henry stayed in the tunnel.

So they gave it up. They told Henry, "We shall leave you there for always and always and always."

They took up the old rails, built a wall in front of him, and cut a new tunnel.

Now Henry can't get out, and he watches the trains rushing through the new tunnel. He is very sad because no one will ever see his lovely green paint with red stripes again.

But I think he deserved it, don't you?

EDWARD, GORDON AND HENRY

Edward and Gordon often went through the tunnel where Henry was shut up.

Edward would say, "Peep, peep – hullo!" and Gordon would say, "Poop, poop, poop! Serves you right!"

Poor Henry had no steam to answer, his fire had gone out; soot and dirt from the tunnel roof had spoilt his lovely green paint and red stripes. He was cold and unhappy, and wanted to come out and pull trains too.

Gordon always pulled the express. He was proud of being the only engine strong enough to do it.

There were many heavy coaches, full of important people like the Fat Director who had punished Henry.

Gordon was seeing how fast he could go. "Hurry! hurry! hurry!" he panted.

"Trickety-trock, trickety-trock, trickety-trock," said the coaches.

Gordon could see Henry's tunnel in front.

"In a minute," he thought, "I'll poop, poop, poop at Henry, and rush through and out into the open again."

Closer and closer he came – he was almost there, when crack: "Wheee————eeshshsh," he was in a cloud of steam, and going slower and slower.

His Driver stopped the train.

"What has happened to me?" asked Gordon, "I feel so weak." "You've burst your safety valve," said the Driver. "You can't pull the train any more." "Oh, dear," said Gordon. "We were going so nicely, too. ... Look at Henry laughing at me." Gordon made a face at Henry, and blew smoke at him.

Everybody got out, and came to see Gordon. "Humph!" said the Fat Director. "I never liked these big engines – always going wrong; send for another engine at once."

While the Guard went to find one, they uncoupled Gordon, and ran him on a siding out of the way.

The only engine left in the shed was Edward.

"I'll come and try," he said.

Gordon saw him coming. "That's no use," he said, "Edward can't pull the train."

Edward puffed and pulled, and pulled and puffed, but he couldn't move the heavy coaches.

"I told you so," said Gordon rudely. "Why not let Henry try?"

"Yes," said the Fat Director, "I will."

"Will you help pull this train, Henry?" he asked. "Yes," said Henry at once.

So Gordon's Driver and Fireman lit his fire; some platelayers broke down the wall and put back the rails; and when he had steam up Henry puffed out.

He was dirty, his boiler was black, and he was covered with cobwebs. "Ooh! I'm so stiff! Ooh! I'm so stiff!" he groaned.

"You'd better have a run to ease your joints, and find a turntable," said the Fat Director kindly.

Henry came back feeling better, and they put him in front.

"Peep, peep," said Edward, "I'm ready."

"Peep, peep, peep," said Henry, "so am I."

"Pull hard; pull hard; pull hard," puffed Edward.

"We'll do it; we'll do it; we'll do it," puffed Henry.

"Pull hard we'll do it. Pull hard we'll do it. Pull hard we'll do it," they puffed together. The heavy coaches jerked and began to move, slowly at first, then faster and faster.

"We've done it together! We've done it together! We've done it together!" said Edward and Henry.

"You've done it, hurray! You've done it, hurray! You've done it, hurray!" sang the coaches.

All the passengers were excited. The Fat Director leaned out of the window to wave to Edward and Henry; but the train was going so fast that his hat blew off into a field where a goat ate it for his tea.

They never stopped till they came to the big station at the end of the line.

The passengers all got out and said, "Thank you," and the Fat Director promised Henry a new coat of paint.

"Would you like blue and red?"

"Yes, please," said Henry, "then I'll be like Edward."

Edward and Henry went home quietly, and on their way they helped Gordon back to the shed.

All three engines are now great friends.

Wasn't Henry pleased when he had his new coat. He is very proud of it, as all good engines are – but he doesn't mind the rain now, because he knows that the best way to keep his paint nice is not to run into tunnels, but to ask his Driver to rub him down when the day's work is over.

Just after this story, the Railways were nationalised and the Fat Director became the Fat Controller.

JAMES THE RED ENGINE
JAMES AND THE TOP-HAT

James was a new engine who lived at a station at the other end of the line. He had two small wheels in front and six driving wheels behind. They weren't as big as Gordon's, and they weren't as small as Thomas's.*

"You're a special Mixed-Traffic engine," the Fat Controller told him. "You'll be able to pull coaches or trucks quite easily."

*Thomas the Tank Engine: a Really Useful Engine whom the Fat Controller has entrusted with his own Branch Line.

But trucks are not easy things to manage and on his first day they had pushed him down a hill into a field.

He had been ill after the accident, but now he had new brakes and a shining coat of red paint.

"The red paint will cheer you up after your accident," said the Fat Controller kindly. "You are to pull coaches today, and Edward shall help you."

They went together to find the coaches.

"Be careful with the coaches, James," said Edward, "they don't like being bumped. Trucks are silly and noisy; they need to be bumped and taught to behave, but coaches get cross and will pay you out."

They took the coaches to the platform and were both coupled on in front. The Fat Controller, the Station Master, and some little boys all came to admire James's shining rods and red paint.

James was pleased. "I am a really splendid engine," he thought, and suddenly let off steam, "Whee—ee—ee—eesh!"

The Fat Controller, the Station Master and the Guard all jumped, and a shower of water fell on the Fat Controller's nice new top-hat.

Just then the whistle blew and James thought they had better go – so they went!

"Go on, go on," he puffed to Edward.

"Don't push, don't push," puffed Edward, for he did not like starting quickly.

"Don't go so fast, don't go so fast," grumbled the coaches; but James did not listen. He wanted to run away before the Fat Controller could call him back.

He didn't even want to stop at the first station. Edward tried hard to stop, but the two coaches in front were beyond the platform before they stopped, and they had to go back to let the passengers get out.

Lots of people came to look at James, and, as no one seemed to know about the Fat Controller's top-hat, James felt happier.

Presently they came to the junction where Thomas was waiting with his two coaches.

"Hullo, James!" said Thomas kindly, "feeling better? That's right. Ah! that's my guard's whistle. I must go. Sorry I can't stop. I don't know what the Fat Controller would do without me to run this branch line," and he puffed off importantly with his two coaches into a tunnel.

Leaving the junction, they passed the field where James had had his accident. The fence was mended and the cows were back again. James whistled, but they paid no attention.

They clattered through Edward's stationyard and started to climb the hill beyond.

"It's ever so steep, it's ever so steep," puffed James.

"I've done it before, I've done it before," puffed Edward.

"It's steep, but we'll do it – it's steep, but we'll do it," the two engines puffed together as they pulled the train up the long hill.

They both rested at the next station; Edward told James how Gordon had stuck on the hill, and he had had to push him up!

James laughed so much that he got hiccoughs and surprised an old lady in a black bonnet.

She dropped all her parcels, and three porters, the Station Master and the Guard had to run after her picking them up!

James was quiet in the shed that night. He had enjoyed his day, but he was a little afraid of what the Fat Controller would say about the top-hat!

James and the Boot-Lace

Next morning the Fat Controller spoke severely to James: "If you can't behave, I shall take away your red coat and have you painted blue."

James did not like that at all and he was very rough with the coaches as he brought them to the platform.

"Come along, come along," he called rudely.

"All in good time, all in good time," the coaches grumbled.

"Don't talk, come on!" answered James, and with the

coaches squealing and grumbling after him, he snorted into the station.

James *was* cross that morning. The Fat Controller had spoken to him, the coaches had dawdled and, worst of all, he had had to fetch his own coaches.

"Gordon never does," thought James, "and he is only painted blue. A splendid Red Engine like me should never have to fetch his own coaches." And he puffed and snorted round to the front of the train, and backed on to it with a rude bump.

"O—ooooh!" groaned the coaches, "that was too bad!"

To make James even more cross, he then had to take the coaches to a different platform, where no one came near him as he stood there. The Fat Controller was in his office, the Station Master was at the other end of the train with the Guard, and even the little boys stood a long way off.

James felt lonely, "I'll show them!" he said to himself. "They think Gordon is the only engine who can pull coaches."

And as soon as the Guard's whistle blew, he started off with a tremendous jerk.

"Come on! — come on! — come on!" he puffed, and the coaches, squeaking and groaning in protest, clattered over the points on to the open line.

"Hurry! — hurry! — hurry!" puffed James.

"You're going too fast, you're going too fast," said the coaches, and indeed they were going so fast that they swayed from side to side.

James laughed and tried to go faster, but the coaches wouldn't let him.

"We're going to stop — we're going to stop — we're —— going —— to —— stop," they said and James found himself going slower and slower.

"What's the matter?" James asked his Driver.

"The brakes are hard on – leak in the pipe most likely. You've banged the coaches enough to make a leak in anything."

The Guard and the Driver got down and looked at the brake pipes all along the train.

At last they found a hole where rough treatment had made a joint work loose.

"How shall we mend it?" said the Guard.

James's Driver thought for a moment.

"We'll do it with newspapers and a leather boot-lace."

"Well, where is the boot-lace coming from?" asked the

Guard. "We haven't one."

"Ask the passengers," said the Driver.

So the Guard made everyone get out.

"Has anybody got a leather boot-lace?" he asked.

They all said "No" except one man in a bowler hat (whose name was Jeremiah Jobling) who tried to hide his feet.

"You have a leather boot-lace there I see, sir," said the Guard. "Please give it to me."

"I won't," said Jeremiah Jobling.

"Then," said the Guard sternly, "I'm afraid this train will just stop where it is."

Then the passengers all told the Guard, the Driver and the Fireman what a Bad Railway it was. But the Guard climbed into his van, and the Driver and Fireman made James let off steam. So they all told Jeremiah Jobling he was a Bad Man instead.

At last he gave them his laces, the Driver tied a pad of newspapers tightly round the hole, and James was able to pull the train.

But he was a sadder and a wiser James and took care never to bump coaches again.

TROUBLESOME TRUCKS

James did not see the Fat Controller for several days. They left James alone in the shed, and did not even allow him to go out and push coaches and trucks in the yard.

"Oh, dear!" he thought sadly, "I'll never be allowed out any more; I shall have to stay in this shed for always, and no one will ever see my red coat again. Oh, dear! Oh, dear!" James began to cry.

Just then the Fat Controller came along.

"I see you are sorry, James," he said. "I hope, now, that you will be a better Engine. You have given me a lot of trouble. People are laughing at my Railway, and I do not like that at all."

"I am very sorry, sir," said James. "I will try hard to behave."

"That's a good engine," said the Fat Controller kindly. "I want you to pull some trucks for me. Run along and find them."

So James puffed happily away.

"Here are your trucks, James," said a little tank engine. "Have you got some boot-laces ready?" And he ran off laughing rudely.

"Oh! Oh! Oh!" said the trucks, as James backed down on them. "We want a proper engine, not a Red Monster."

James took no notice and started as soon as the guard was ready.

"Come along, come along," he puffed.

"We won't! We won't!" screamed the trucks.

But James didn't care, and he pulled the screeching trucks sternly out of the yard.

The trucks tried hard to make him give up, but he still kept on.

Sometimes their brakes would slip "on", and sometimes their axles would "run hot". Each time they would have to stop and put the trouble right, and each time James would start again, determined not to let the trucks beat him.

"Give up! give up! you can't pull us! You can't! You can't!" called the trucks.

"I can and I will! I can and I will!" puffed James.

And slowly but surely he pulled them along the line.

At last they saw Gordon's hill ahead.

"Look out for trouble, James," warned his Driver. "We'll go fast and get them up before they know it. Don't let them stop you."

So James went faster, and they were soon halfway up the hill.

"I'm doing it! I'm doing it!" he panted.

But it was hard work.

"Will the top never come?" he thought, when with a sudden jerk it all came easier.

"I've done it! I've done it!" he puffed triumphantly.

"Hurrah!" he thought, "it's easy now." But his Driver shut off steam.

"They've done it again," he said. —"We've left our tail behind!"

The last ten trucks were running backwards down the hill. The coupling had snapped!

But the Guard was brave. Very carefully and cleverly he made them stop. Then he got out and walked down the line with his red flag.

"That's why it was easy," said James as he backed the other trucks carefully down. "What silly things trucks are! There might have been an accident."

Meanwhile the Guard had stopped Edward who was pulling three coaches.

"Shall I help you, James?" called Edward.

"No, thank you," answered James, "I'll pull them myself."

"Good, don't let them beat you."

So James got ready. Then with a "peep, peep" he was off.

"I *can* do it, I *can* do it," he puffed. He pulled and puffed as hard as he could.

"Peep pip peep peep! You're doing well!" whistled Edward, as James slowly struggled up the hill, with clouds of smoke and steam pouring from his funnel.

"I've done it, I've done it," he panted and disappeared over the top.

They reached their station safely. James was resting in the yard, when Edward puffed by with a cheerful "peep peep".

Then, walking towards him across the rails, James saw . . . the Fat Controller!

"Oh dear! What will he say?" he asked himself sadly.

But the Fat Controller was smiling. "I was in Edward's train, and saw everything," he said. "You've made the most troublesome trucks on the line behave. After that, you deserve to keep your red coat."

JAMES AND THE EXPRESS

Sometimes Gordon and Henry slept in James's shed, and they would talk of nothing but boot-laces! James would talk about engines who got shut up in tunnels and stuck on hills, but they wouldn't listen, and went on talking and laughing.

"You talk too much, little James," Gordon would say. "A fine strong engine like me has something to talk about. I'm the only engine who can pull the Express. When I'm not there, they need two engines. Think of that!"

"I've pulled expresses for years, and have never once lost my way. I seem to know the right line by instinct," said Gordon proudly. Every wise engine knows, of course, that the signalman works the points to make engines run on the right lines, but Gordon was so proud that he had forgotten.

"Wake up, James," he said next morning, "it's nearly time for the Express. What are you doing? – Odd jobs? Ah well! We all have to begin somewhere, don't we? Run along now and get my coaches – don't be late now."

James went to get Gordon's coaches. They were now all shining with lovely new paint. He was careful not to bump them, and they followed him smoothly into the station singing happily. "We're going away, we're going away."

"I wish I was going with you," said James. "I should love to pull the Express and go flying along the line."

He left them in the station and went back to the yard, just as Gordon with much noise and blowing of steam backed on to the train.

The Fat Controller was on the train with other Important People, and, as soon as they heard the guard's whistle, Gordon started.

"Look at me now! Look at me now!" he puffed, and the coaches glided after him out of the station.

"Poop poop poo poo poop! – Good-bye little James! See you tomorrow."

James watched the train disappear round a curve, and then went back to work. He pushed some trucks into their proper sidings and went to fetch the coaches for another train.

He brought the coaches to the platform and was just being uncoupled when he heard a mournful, quiet "Shush shush shush shush!" and there was Gordon trying to sidle into the station without being noticed.

"Hullo, Gordon! Is it tomorrow?" asked James. Gordon didn't answer; he just let off steam feebly.

"Did you lose your way, Gordon?"

"No, it was lost for me," he answered crossly, "I was switched off the main line on to the loop; I had to go all round and back again."

"Perhaps it was instinct," said James brightly.

Meanwhile all the passengers hurried to the booking office. "We want our money back," they shouted.

Everyone was making a noise, but the Fat Controller climbed on a trolley and blew the Guard's whistle so loudly that they all stopped to look at him.

Then he promised them a new train at once.

"Gordon can't do it," he said. "Will you pull it for us, James?"

"Yes, sir, I'll try."

So James was coupled on and everyone got in again.

"Do your best, James," said the Fat Controller kindly. Just then the whistle blew and he had to run to get in.

"Come along, come along," puffed James.

"You're pulling us well! you're pulling us well," sang the coaches.

"Hurry, hurry, hurry," puffed James.

Stations and bridges flashed by, the passengers leaned out of the windows and cheered, and they soon reached the terminus.

Everyone said "Thank you" to James. "Well done," said the Fat Controller. "Would you like to pull the Express sometimes?"

"Yes, please," answered James happily.

Next day when James came by, Gordon was pushing trucks in the yard.

"I like some quiet work for a change," he said. "I'm teaching these trucks manners. You did well with those coaches I hear ... good, we'll show them!" and he gave his trucks a bump, making them cry, "Oh! Oh! Oh! Oh!"

James and Gordon are now good friends. James sometimes takes the Express to give Gordon a rest. Gordon never talks about boot-laces, and they are both quite agreed on the subject of trucks!

TROUBLESOME ENGINES
HENRY AND THE ELEPHANT

Henry and Gordon were lonely when Thomas left the yard to run his Branch Line. They missed him very much.

They had more work to do. They couldn't wait in the shed till it was time, and find their coaches at the platform; they had to fetch them. They didn't like that.

Edward sometimes did odd jobs, and so did James, but James soon started grumbling too. The Fat Controller kindly gave Henry and Gordon new coats of paint (Henry chose green), but they still grumbled dreadfully.

"We get no rest, we get no rest," they complained as they clanked about the Yard; but the coaches only laughed.

"You're lazy and slack, you're lazy and slack," they answered in their quiet, rude way.

But when a Circus came to town, the engines forgot they were tired. They all wanted to shunt the special trucks and coaches.

They were dreadfully jealous of James when the Fat Controller told him to pull the train when the Circus went away.

However, they soon forgot about the animals as they had plenty of work to do.

One morning Henry was told to take some workmen to a tunnel which was blocked.

He grumbled away to find two trucks to carry the workmen and their tools.

"Pushing trucks! Pushing trucks!" he muttered in a sulky sort of way.

They stopped outside the tunnel, and tried to look through it, but it was quite dark; no daylight shone from the other end.

The workmen took their tools and went inside.

Suddenly with a shout they all ran out looking frightened.

"We went to the block and started to dig, but it grunted and moved," they said.

"Rubbish," said the foreman.

"It's not rubbish, it's big and alive; we're not going in there again."

"Right," said the foreman, "I'll ride in a truck and Henry shall push it out."

"Wheeeesh," said Henry unhappily. He hated tunnels (he had been shut up in one once), but this was worse; something big and alive was inside.

"Peep pep peep pip pip pee—eep!" he whistled, "I don't want to go in!"

"Neither do I," said his Driver, "but we must clear the line."

"Oh dear! Oh dear!" puffed Henry as they slowly advanced into the darkness.

B U M P————!!!!

Henry's driver shut off steam at once.

"Help! Help! we're going back," wailed Henry, and slowly moving out into the daylight came first Henry, then the trucks, and last of all, pushing hard and rather cross, came a large elephant.

"Well I never did!" said the foreman. "It's an elephant from the Circus."

Henry's Driver put on his brakes, and a man ran to telephone for the keeper.

The elephant stopped pushing and came towards them. They gave him some sandwiches and cake, so he forgot he was cross and remembered he was hungry. He drank three buckets of water without stopping, and was just going to drink another when Henry let off steam.

The elephant jumped, and "hoo——oosh", he squirted the water over Henry by mistake.

Poor Henry!

When the keeper came, the workmen rode home happily in the trucks, laughing at their adventure, but Henry was very cross.

"An elephant pushed me! an elephant hooshed me!" he hissed.

He was sulky all day, and his coaches had an uncomfortable time.

In the shed he told Gordon and James about the elephant, and I am sorry to say that instead of laughing and telling him not to be silly, they looked sad and said:

"You poor engine, you have been badly treated."

TENDERS AND TURNTABLES

The big stations at both ends of the line each have a turntable. The Fat Controller had them made so that Edward, Henry, Gordon and James can be turned round. It is dangerous for Tender Engines to go fast backwards. Tank Engines like Thomas don't need turntables; they can go just as well backwards as forwards.

But if you had heard Gordon talking a short while ago, you would have thought that the Fat Controller had given him a tender just to show how important he was.

"You don't understand, little Thomas," said Gordon, "we Tender Engines have a position to keep up. You haven't a Tender and that makes a difference. It doesn't matter where *you* go, but We are Important, and for the Fat Controller to make us shunt trucks, fetch coaches and go on some of those dirty sidings it's—— it's—— well it's not the Proper Thing."

And Gordon puffed away in a dignified manner.

Thomas chuckled and went off with Annie and Clarabel.

Arrived at the Terminus, Gordon waited till all the passengers had got out; then, groaning and grumbling, he shunted the coaches to another platform.

"Disgraceful! Disgraceful!" he hissed as he ran backwards to the turntable.

The turntable was in a windy place close to the sea. It was only just big enough for Gordon, and if he was not on it just right, he put it out of balance, and made it difficult to turn.

Today, Gordon was in a bad temper, and the wind was blowing fiercely.

His Driver tried to make him stop in the right place; backwards and forwards they went, but Gordon wasn't trying.

At last Gordon's Driver gave it up. The Fireman tried to turn the handle, but Gordon's weight and the strong wind prevented him. The Driver, some platelayers, and the Fireman all tried together.

"It's no good," they said at last, mopping their faces, "your tender upsets the balance. If you were a nice Tank Engine, you'd be all right. Now you'll have to pull the next train backwards."

Gordon came to the platform. Some little boys shouted, "Come on quick, here's a new Tank Engine."

"What a swiz!" they said, when they came near, "it's only Gordon, back to front."

Gordon hissed emotionally.

He puffed to the junction. "Hullo!" called Thomas, "playing Tank Engines? Sensible engine! Take my advice, scrap your tender and have a nice bunker instead."

Gordon snorted, but didn't answer. Even James laughed when he saw him. "Take care," hissed Gordon, "you might stick too."

"No fear," chuckled James, "I'm not so fat as you."

"I mustn't stick," thought James anxiously, as he ran to the turntable later. He stopped on just the right place to balance the table. It could now swing easily. His Fireman turned the handle . . . James turned . . . much too easily! The wind puffed him round like a top. He couldn't stop! . . .

At last the wind died down, and James stopped turning, but not before Gordon, who had been turned on the loop line, had seen him.

"Well! Well!" he said, "are you playing roundabouts?"

Poor James, feeling quite giddy, rolled off to the shed without a word.

That night the three engines had an "indignation meeting".

"It's shameful to treat Tender Engines like this! Henry gets 'hooshed' by elephants; Gordon has to go backwards and people think he's a Tank Engine. James spins round like a top, and everyone laughs at us. And added to that, the Fat Controller makes us shunt in dirty sidings. Ugh ————!!" said all three engines together.

"Listen," said Gordon. . . . He whispered something to the others: "We'll do it tomorrow. The Fat Controller *will* look silly!"

Trouble in the Shed

The Fat Controller sat in his office and listened. The Fat Controller frowned and said, "What a nuisance passengers are! How can I work with all this noise?"

The Station Master knocked and came in, looking worried.

"There's trouble in the shed, Sir. Henry is sulking; there is no train, and the Passengers are saying this is a Bad Railway."

"Indeed!" said the Fat Controller. "We cannot allow that. Will you quieten the passengers, please; I will go and speak to Henry."

He found Henry, Gordon and James looking sulky.

"Come along, Henry," he said, "it is time your train was ready."

"Henry's not going," said Gordon rudely. "We *won't* shunt like Common Tank Engines. We are Important Tender Engines. You fetch our coaches and we will pull them. Tender Engines don't shunt," and all three engines let off steam in a cheeky way.

"Oh indeed," said the Fat Controller severely. "We'll see about that; engines on My Railway do as they are told."

He hurried away, climbed into his car and drove to find Edward.

"The Yard has never been the same since Thomas left," he thought sadly.

Edward was shunting.

"Leave those trucks please, Edward; I want you to push coaches for me in the Yard."

"Thank you, Sir, that will be a nice change."

"That's a good engine," said the Fat Controller kindly, "off you go then."

So Edward found coaches for the three engines, and that day the trains ran as usual.

But when the Fat Controller came next morning, Edward looked unhappy.

Gordon came clanking past, hissing rudely. "Bless me!" said the Fat Controller. "What a noise!"

"They all hiss me, Sir," answered Edward sadly. "They say 'Tender Engines don't shunt', and last night they said I had black wheels. I haven't, have I, Sir?"

"No, Edward, you have nice blue ones, and I'm proud of you. Tender Engines do shunt, but all the same you'd be happier in your own Yard. We need a Tank Engine here."

He went to an Engine Workshop, and they showed him all sorts of Tank Engines. There were big ones, and little ones; some looked happy, and some sad, and some looked at him anxiously, hoping he would choose them.

At last he saw a smart little green engine with four wheels.

"That's the one," he thought.

"If I choose you, will you work hard?"

"Oh Sir! Yes Sir!"

"That's a good engine; I'll call you Percy."

"Yes Sir! Thank you Sir!" said Percy happily.

So he bought Percy and drove him back to the Yard.

"Edward," he called, "here's Percy; will you show him everything?"

Percy soon learned what he had to do, and they had a happy afternoon.

Once Henry came by hissing as usual.

"Whee——eesh!" said Percy suddenly; Henry jumped and ran back to the shed.

"How beautifully you wheeshed him," laughed Edward. "I can't wheesh like that."

"Oh!" said Percy modestly, "that's nothing; you should hear them in the workshop. You have to wheesh loudly to make yourself heard."

Next morning Thomas arrived. "The Fat Controller sent for me; I expect he wants help," he said importantly to Edward.

"Sh! Sh! here he comes."

"Well done Thomas; you've been quick. Listen, Henry, Gordon and James are sulking; they say they won't shunt like Common Tank Engines. So I have shut them up, and I want you both to run the line."

"Common Tank Engines indeed!" snorted Thomas. "We'll show them."

"And Percy here will help too," said the Fat Controller.

"Oh Sir! Yes Sir! Please Sir!" answered Percy excitedly.

Edward and Thomas worked the line. Starting at opposite ends, they pulled the trains, whistling cheerfully to each other as they passed.

Percy sometimes puffed along the Branch Line. Thomas was anxious, but both Driver and Guard promised to take care of Annie and Clarabel.

There were fewer trains, but the Passengers didn't mind; they knew the three other engines were having a Lesson.

Henry, Gordon and James stayed shut in the shed, and were cold, lonely and miserable. They wished now they hadn't been so silly.

PERCY RUNS AWAY

Henry, Gordon and James were shut up for several days. At last the Fat Controller opened the shed.

"I hope you are sorry," he said sternly, "and understand you are not so important after all. Thomas, Edward and Percy have worked the Line very nicely. They need a change, and I will let you out if you promise to be good."

"Yes Sir!" said the three engines, "we will."

"That's right, but please remember that this 'no shunting' nonsense must stop."

He told Edward, Thomas and Percy that they could go and play on the Branch Line for a few days.

They ran off happily and found Annie and Clarabel at the Junction. The two coaches were so pleased to see Thomas again, and he took them for a run at once. Edward and Percy played with trucks.

"Stop! Stop! Stop!" screamed the trucks as they were pushed into their proper sidings, but the two engines laughed and went on shunting till the trucks were tidily arranged.

Next, Edward took some empty trucks to the Quarry, and Percy was left alone.

Percy didn't mind that a bit; he liked watching trains and being cheeky to the engines.

"Hurry! Hurry! Hurry!" he would call to them. Gordon, Henry and James got very cross!

After a while he took some trucks over the main line to another siding. When they were tidy, he ran on to the main line again, and waited for the signalman to set the points so that he could cross back to the Yard.

Edward had warned Percy: "Be careful on the Main Line; whistle to tell the signalman you are there."

But Percy didn't remember to whistle, and the signalman was so busy, and forgot Percy.

Bells rang in the signal box; the man answered, saying the line was clear, and set the signals for the next train.

Percy waited and waited; the points were still against him. He looked along the Main Line ... "Peep! Peep!" he whistled in horror for, rushing straight towards him, was Gordon with the Express.

"Poop poop poo-poo-poop!" whistled Gordon. His Driver shut off steam and applied the brakes.

Percy's Driver turned on full steam. "Back Percy! Back!" he urged; but Percy's wheel wouldn't turn quickly. Gordon was coming so fast that it seemed he couldn't stop. With shut eyes Percy waited for the crash. His Driver and Fireman jumped out.

"Oo——ooh e——er!" groaned Gordon. "Get out of my way."

Percy opened his eyes; Gordon had stopped with Percy's buffers a few inches from his own.

But Percy had begun to move. "I — won't stay — here — I'll — run — a — way," he puffed. He was soon clear of the station and running as fast as he could. He went through Edward's station whistling loudly, and was so frightened that he ran right up Gordon's hill without stopping.

He was tired then, and wanted to stop, but he couldn't . . . he had no Driver to shut off steam and to apply the brakes.

"I shall have to run till my wheels wear out," he thought sadly. "Oh dear! Oh dear!"

"I — want — to — stop, I — want — to — stop," he puffed in a tired sort of way.

He passed another signal box. "I know just what you want, little Percy," called the man kindly. He set the points, and Percy puffed wearily on to a nice empty siding ending in a big bank of earth.

Percy was too tired now to care where he went. "I — want — to — stop, I — want — to — stop ——— I — *have* — stopped!" he puffed thankfully, as his bunker buried itself in the bank.

"Never mind, Percy," said the workmen as they dug him out, "you shall have a drink and some coal, and then you'll feel better."

Presently Gordon arrived.

"Well done Percy, you started so quickly that you stopped a nasty accident."

'I'm sorry I was cheeky," said Percy, "you were clever to stop."

Percy now works in the Yard and finds coaches for the trains. He is still cheeky because he is that sort of engine, but he is always *most* careful when he goes on the Main Line.

The End